ULTIMATE HACK

LANCE ERLICK

Finlee Augare Books (Chicago)

This is a work of fiction. All of the characters, organizations, and events portrayed herein are either products of the author's imagination or are used fictitiously, and any similarities to actual persons, organizations, or events is entirely coincidental. Also, though locations used in this work exist, for dramatic effect details have been altered. Accordingly, they should be considered fictitious.

Finlee Augare Books, Chicago, IL
ISBN: 978-1-943080-28-1 (print)
ISBN: 978-1-943080-29-8 (e-book)

Printed in the United States of America

ONE

Hercules launched his one-hundred-thirty-seventh electronic probe. Maybe this one would penetrate the fifth firewall on Krill Metal Enterprises' private server.

Weary from a week with little sleep, he scooted his chair away from the six flat screens that lined the basement wall. He stood to stretch and tripped over the battery backup sump-pump, the one he'd talked his mom into installing to protect his equipment.

In the process of steadying himself, he knocked over the king on a nearby chessboard. This was where he tested new strategies for the matches he played on World Champion Games Online. He hadn't made a move in over a week. In fact, he hadn't left his mom's basement in all that time.

He replaced the king, tried to ignore the bad omen, and sat down. While waiting to see what his probe produced, he rummaged through foil junk-food bags for something to tide him over. The power bars had disappeared days earlier, along with the cookies and pretzels.

"What's going on down there?" his mom yelled from the top of the stairs. Her shrill voice rang in his ears. "Did something crash?"

Hercules sank lower in his seat. "It's nothing, Mom."

"It didn't sound like nothing. Are you drinking again?"

His mom slung loaded questions to trip him up, since "no" admitted that he had been drinking before. *Not at home.* "I'm not drinking, Mom."

"Aren't you going to work today?"

"I am working." *Just not on my boring intern job.*

"Come have breakfast first. You haven't eaten a proper meal in a week. You're too skinny to skip food. You're not doing drugs down there, are you?" his mom yelled, *as if a druggie might confess.*

Maybe to get the nagging to stop. "No, Mom."

Hercules had no use for anything that dulled his mind, which ached from a puzzle far beyond the chess or other hacking challenges: how to see what Krill was hiding. "I need to concentrate." He hoped that would send her away for a while.

After all, eating was a waste of time, except to stop his belly from grumbling. He emptied the crumbs from some cookie bags into his mouth and looked around. After a week, he'd scrounged all the food he'd brought downstairs and his mom refused to buy more until he joined her for a "proper" meal.

Hercules, not his real name, drummed his fingers on his virtual keyboard, as if that could speed things up. At least it diverted attention from his empty stomach and how he'd failed to penetrate Krill's last layer of security.

He'd used every tool in his library, including the contents of both hard drives attached to his system and the ones he'd locked in a fireproof safe on a bowed plastic shelf because he didn't trust centralize cloud databases. Rational thought begged him to give up this quest.

A dead-end after weeks of work would be devastating, but something inside him wouldn't let go. Okay, the challenge of breaking firewalls others couldn't was a thrill, but it was more than that. Each night when his head hit the pillow in the far corner of the basement, this inner force plagued him with the incongruity of the tightest security he'd encountered for such a mundane company doing routine boring metal fabrication.

The biggest mental pest was Simeon. Hercules knew little about the hacker legend: not country, age, or even gender. Simeon was a god in the dark corners of the virtual world: faceless, voiceless, a ghost to those who pursued him/her. S/he was also Hercules' mentor, the one who introduced him to a network of brothers and sisters who helped him find niche code and special purpose hacks.

"You can find anything you need on skull-and-crossbones sites," Simeon had texted, using a filter to remove any personal quirks to fool those with sophisticated language analyzers. "But be careful. There are crazy Jackers out here."

Jackers were like hackers except they got into your head to mess you up. That was enough reason to hide behind false names, faces, and profiles. In any case, Simeon's last mission was Krill Metal Enterprises. Then s/he'd vanished.

Simeon didn't just disappear as in never heard from again. All electronic traces of him/her vanished, as if s/he'd never existed. That hit Hercules like a kick to the gut. The vanishing act had reminded him of how his father abandoned his family two years ago for a girl right out of high school, and a job in another country.

Despite Daddy's fancy executive job and top one-tenth-of-one-percenter paycheck, he'd pleaded poverty. Dear old Dad paid only what the courts could get from him. Then he vanished off the grid. The payments stopped, leaving Hercules and his mom struggling to get by. Ever since, Hercules had been hunting his deadbeat dad in secure databases and behind secure corporate firewalls.

This driving need, alter ego, or hacker demon—take your pick—which he couldn't share with family or friends, spurred Hercules to uncover what had happened to

Simeon as a way to learn more about how his dad vanished. Somehow, he decided, these mysteries related to what the mundane company was hiding. Even the registered owner's name, John Jones, was an alias, with no public information. Hercules was certain he was a top earning one-tenth-of-one-percenter like his father.

Spurred by the hunt for his dad, Hercules became a self-proclaimed champion of transparency, hoping to spare others the pain of lies and deceit. He vowed to uncover Krill's secrets and publicize them on his website, the Labors of Hercules, as he'd done with others before. If he was lucky, he'd find clues to locating his dad.

Krill's tight security had to cover some hideous stench. Hercules might find a buyer for the secrets if doing so didn't violate his moral compass: don't hurt people trampled by big companies and the rich. Impersonal corporations and their lackeys were fair game. He wasn't selling out for the money. He used all proceeds to buy equipment to continue his mission.

A screen to his right held the private image of another rail-thin boy in a dirty tee shirt and ragged jeans: Hercules' partner, Apollo. The boy sported a week's worth of beard beneath uncombed sandy hair. Few, other than Hercules, could connect the Apollo screen name to this quiet, private figure or his real name, Paulo Antonelli. It seemed a poor alias for someone who hid in the shadows and didn't aspire to greatness, but it was easy for his friend to remember.

As part of their friendship and collaboration, Hercules and Apollo had set up reciprocal cameras in their home offices in case either got into trouble. After all, they were digging into very secure data systems. Like Apollo, Hercules had changed his name according to the French greeting, which literally asked, "What do you call yourself?" The English equivalent, "What's your name?" sounded like: "What label did others slap on you?"

To succeed in his mission, Hercules needed one more

mutation of a probe bot that the Krill firewall wouldn't recognize. Apollo knew how to create small data packets to drill through impossible security. He hadn't hit a system he couldn't crack. Yet Apollo was sweating so much he'd draped a towel around his neck. Empty foil bags littered the table around him and tumbled onto the floor. Despite the sweat, Apollo didn't appear to be drinking. No mugs or plastic containers were in sight.

"You okay?" Hercules asked into the microphone.

Apollo stared at his virtual keyboard in the corner of his bedroom. His hands trembled. When he spoke, words came out slow and methodical as if he'd chewed on them for hours. "No, man, I'm not." He brushed aside foil bags, dropping crumbs on the virtual keyboard. Gibberish flashed across his screen as it executed Python code in response to the crumbs dancing across the tabletop. Apollo scooped the rest of the crumbs into his hand and popped them into his mouth.

Another screen showed Apollo's public image. A small humanlike figure of the Greek god held the world above his head. The contrast between public and private images drew a tear to Hercules' eyes. It tugged at his sense of injustice to think of how his decent friend had been bullied one time too many for being shy, slow of speech, and socially awkward.

To avoid pushing his friend too hard, Hercules softened his voice, though he couldn't contain his enthusiasm. "Come on, dude. It's the hack of a lifetime. We could nail another shady one-percenter."

"Enough."

"You're the best," Hercules said. "I'm counting on you. You'll be a hero."

"Save it, man. You've gone wacky over this. You know that? Wacky. This isn't fun anymore. We could get into serious trouble." Apollo used his sleeve to clean the table and then typed to fix the garbage on his screen.

Apollo hadn't been as eager to take on the one-percenter cause. Then Hercules hooked him up with their summer internship at XTEL Development, which allowed them to work from home. The job was only between high school and their backup plan of going to college. And that was only if they couldn't support themselves by hacking.

The intern program was supposed to give them skills to help in college or to get a real, full-time job. So far the internship hadn't taught Hercules squat, but their servers held a lot of interesting stuff, such as salaries and client firewall protocols.

He resented doing menial work for a boss who was more interested in hitting on female interns than in giving the interns real work. Conrad Jackson was another home-wrecker, with money and an apartment hidden from his wife, according to his many bank records. Conrad also owned stock in a company with a name similar to Krill Metal Enterprises, though all shell companies sounded alike. Still, the intern job was a useful cover to keep Hercules' mom from bugging him when he was home.

"Come on, Apollo," Hercules said in the most soothing tone he could manage. "You're a god. A top god."

"One more word and I'll pull the plug." Apollo pointed to a tiny icon on his screen.

The image was too small and far away for Hercules' camera to pick out any details. "Is that the code?"

"I'm warning you. Give this up before the Feds pound on our doors. You want to spend the rest of your life in Area 51?"

"That's for aliens, dude. Besides, this isn't government."

"Go away." Apollo reached over to turn off the camera and mike.

"Don't," Hercules said. "I'll leave you alone. Just don't quit on me." He returned his attention to the probe he'd sent out. Nothing yet.

* * *

On another screen, also with reciprocal cameras, was the image of Dido, Amanda Jains, another co-intern at XTEL, and the third member of their hacker partnership. She refused to say if she'd taken her alias from a popular singer or from Aeneas' mythical lover. That Dido ended up killing herself when Aeneas left her to complete his mission, which made her an unattractive namesake to Hercules' thinking. But Amanda was a romantic who loved to act mysterious.

The biggest mystery to Hercules, despite rationalizations he'd told himself, was why Dido liked him; at least she said she did. Although they'd gone to the same school, they met on a hacker chat-room. She'd impressed him with her playfulness and her ability to break certain private-key codes. They should have been nearly impossible to crack except for the most determined brute-force attacks, but she'd found anomalies that greatly reduced the task.

She'd called him cute, even before they'd met in person. She certainly was, though her baggy clothes rarely showed it.

When he'd let slip that he found her gorgeous as a goddess, she'd laughed. "You say the sweetest things so I'll help you hack."

They fought, kissed, and made up, as if it was all a playful game to her. To his knowledge, she had no other boyfriends, yet dangled mysteries surrounding what attracted her to him. She let him lead on XTEL or transparency projects, knowing that he'd get stumped and come to her as the best code decryptor he knew.

"Am I the only one who knows how good you are?" he'd asked her last week as they left XTEL's offices.

"Our little secret." Dido winked and kissed him on the cheek.

The screen to his right showed the back of her silky cinnamon hair, pulled up in a pony tail. He was lucky to get to see Dido every day, since her mom didn't like him hanging around. He could almost imagine that they were in the same room, as if they were virtual roommates. He would rather have watched Dido's face, but she'd hidden the camera in the wall behind her so her mom wouldn't find it.

Dido liked to tease that she could see him behind her. The thought that she might be studying him on the screen to her left made his hands tremble. His heart skipped a beat. He couldn't tell if she was mad at him, ignoring him, or just absorbed with solving a decryption problem. With better camera resolution, he could have seen himself on her screen along with his screen watching her, like the million images from putting two mirrors facing each other.

Dido sat at her computer beside her bed in her mom's attic, paneled to cover the rafters. It was a bed Hercules longed to return to. After he reached his prize he could leave these distractions behind and give Dido the attention she deserved.

Hercules had invited her over that morning.

"I won't crawl into your wretched dungeon," she'd said.

"I'll clean it up."

She pouted. "Why don't you come up here instead?"

"I need my high speed link. Besides, your system still has a security glitch."

"Then launch your probes and come over to fix it." Her eyes teased him through the screen.

"I can't risk leaving my computer idle. If I turn it off, the probes may bounce back and disappear."

"Just today," Dido had said, in the sweetest voice. "You need a break. You haven't eaten, have you?"

What he needed was a successful probe. "If I don't find anything, I'll come over tonight."

"Maybe I won't be here." She turned off the screen with his image, and returned her attention to her work. It was her way of punishing him by saying she no longer saw him.

Twinges of jealousy gripped Hercules over their XTEL boss' interest in her. Hercules couldn't help feeling she encouraged such speculation to stir him up inside. Whether she did or didn't, it was working.

* * *

Despite what he'd told Dido, Hercules was tempted to shut down his computer, risk losing the probe's connection, and go to her. He'd been neglecting her this past week. He couldn't help it. Krill reminded him of their boss, Conrad Jackson, a corporate man with big toys. And Conrad the womanizer reminded Hercules of his father.

Hercules' breath caught, he struggled to suck in air. His throat tightened. A migraine threatened to blind him. If he hadn't already launched the latest probe, he would have gone to Dido right then. She knew how to help him clear his head. In fact, she'd gotten him to tell her everything about his father, down to the last detail of catching the old man in bed with a blonde two years older than Hercules, a girl he'd looked up to until that night.

He shuddered at the image burned into this brain of his naked father on top of the unclothed girl. The blonde glared at him with a look both innocent and worldly, mixed with anger at the interruption. Stunned, he'd lingered, unable to absorb what he was seeing. It wasn't until later when he couldn't sleep that reality sank in. If he could have rebooted his brain to wipe clean those images he would have. Instead, that picture popped up like unwelcome ads on the Internet.

When the probe returns, he told himself. *No matter what it finds, I'll surprise Dido. Take her to our favorite spot on the lake for a swim. Just the two of us.*

In the meantime, he puzzled over where he was going wrong, and whether his efforts were futile. If this company turned out to be nothing more than what it claimed to be,

Hercules stood to embarrass himself for having pushed Apollo and Dido to help.

Even so, he couldn't stop seeing Krill's layers of security, like the layers of lies and deceptions his father used to hide his affair. The late nights weren't for work. Mid-week business trips were to shack up with the blonde. It had been a fluke that Hercules skipped school the day his mom visited her sister and his dad decided to save a buck on hotel rooms.

That day his father's web of dirty secrets unraveled and the facade of normalcy collapsed. He moved out. Over the next weeks, Hercules replayed every word out of his father's mouth, right down to his dad pleading that they didn't have money while he lavished gifts on his girlfriend.

After the old man vanished, Hercules vowed to track him down using his corporate hacks. Someone had to know where the bastard had gone. But how do you find a ghost?

In the meantime he dug into suspicious corporations to expose their deceptions. Two months ago on dark-net chat rooms, several people exposed a local power station dumping pollutants into a nearby river. Other hackers either couldn't dig into this or weren't motivated. Since this was in Hercules' neighborhood, he dug in.

With Dido's ability to decrypt secure codes, Apollo's electronic drills, and AI bots downloaded from the dark-net, they slipped into the company's secure servers. Hercules didn't expect much. After all, if you committed a crime, you dumped the evidence. Yet he uncovered records and emails tracing every action for their attorneys, something about attorney-client privilege.

Hercules broke the story, releasing records to the press and to the EPA. No one responded. The company's attorneys made sure of that.

Unwilling to give up, he broke stories about tax evasion, marital infidelity, and outright fraud by the company's officers, which he posted on his foreign-hosted website: Labors of Hercules. He sent links to spouses, coworkers, and customers. The company replaced all named officers and announced plans to clean up the environment. The power of transparency was holding people accountable as no one did to his dad.

Last month, Dido helped him crack secure DOD codes. With those, they penetrated a Department of Defense site to expose plans to use drone strikes against terrorists in a new location in Africa. Apollo's electronic drills threatened to override the drones' navigation if the DOD didn't come clean. Hercules posted this information on his website, which promptly crashed. Even so, the military scrapped the drone strikes pending an investigation.

Then counter-probes surfaced, tracing how Hercules and his team had sent signals to threaten a secure military operation. The Department of Defense didn't like that kind of transparency.

Working around the clock, Dido helped him crack into several foreign databases while Apollo's drilling probes severed links and scrambled traces of their activities. They barely destroyed the last connection on a Bangladeshi database before the Feds could trace the feeds back to Hercules.

Each night for the next two weeks he was plagued with nightmares of a knock at the door, handcuffs, and the worse part, a cell with no Internet access. Apollo threatened to quit. Dido warned Hercules to stop charging at windmills. Hercules had to admit he felt as paranoid as they did, but bravery was pursuing the target even when all else warned you to retreat. At least he'd read that somewhere.

Last week, after dark-net chat-room noise peaked over Simeon and Krill Metal Enterprises, Hercules hit a wall trying to tackle Krill's security on his own. He asked for Dido's help with a tricky bit of encryption.

She balked. "I'm tired of coding, tired of staring at the

screen. You've taken the fun out of this. You've turned it into a boring job."

"We owe it to Simeon," Hercules said.

"You don't even know Simeon." She glared at Hercules with suspicious eyes.

Hercules didn't know Simeon yet felt he did. On the off chance Simeon was female, he let it drop. He didn't want to awaken any jealousy in Dido over a hacker he would never meet. "You can crack codes few others can. I need you."

"I want out of this humid attic. It's like having a hairdryer shooting hot mist in my face. Why don't you ever take me places like you used to? Like a real boyfriend?"

"Dido, you know—"

"Save it. At least a movie theater would be cooler. We could go wall-climbing at the mall. There's a dance at the community center tomorrow night."

He couldn't risk telling her how lame a community center dance sounded. He felt too embarrassed. Despite his assumed name, Hercules had two left feet. Or maybe God had put them on backward. He couldn't dance or climb and was too mortified to let Dido see him stumble around like a ridiculous clown.

In any case he'd said, "This is the big one. Trust me. We crack this and I'll take you to a dozen movies." Actually, he found most movies boring. They added too much Hollywood glamour from another bunch of rich one-percenters hiding behind their public masks.

His security probe was taking too long. He'd routed the electronic code through a hack into a nearby network hub, bounced the probe off other hubs, and then spoofed his address as if it came from overseas. Even accounting for that, this was slow, which encouraged him that he might crack another layer of security and download some real files.

Most of what he'd learned about Krill was boring: they bought and sold metal parts. *One more layer*, he told himself. Then he'd have the juicy stuff.

Hercules received a message from another XTEL intern: *Hey Zak-Bak. Y U not at work? Need help finding that new statistics file. Randy.*

Hercules' optical pathways threatened to short-circuit him into blindness over a mutation of a name he couldn't stand. He hated Zackary, Bakke, and the nickname students and interns saddled him with. If he'd had the body of Hercules, he could have put a stop to the name-bashing, though saying anything made the taunting worse.

Zak-Bak coughed at his tablet-phone, as if to transmit the germs. He texted the location of the file any imbecile could have found and signed off: *Sick day.*

With no reply to his probe, Hercules returned his attention to Dido. She was right. He should have packed it in for the day and played hooky with her. They could have found some place to hang out. After all, they both enjoyed walks through the woods down by the lake. Instead, he'd badgered her and Apollo to work on this seemingly unbreakable security shield.

Yet he couldn't let it go. He had to do this for Simeon.

Dido rose from her computer. Hercules held his breath, hoping she was finished, that she'd created a tool to penetrate a Schaeffer Wall, the toughest security he'd come across yet. Instead of sending the file, she turned off his camera feed, blinding him to the space around her computer. This was a breach of their agreement, beyond turning off his screen.

"Dido, you okay?"

She didn't respond, probably turned off the speakers as well. Hercules scowled and tried to recall whether he'd heard a knock. He replayed the recording and froze. There it was: a soft knock he'd missed while texting with Randy.

Hercules pulled up a separate feed from a camera in a

cute porcelain cat he'd given Dido out of concern that someone might break into the attic and hurt her. He figured she knew about the second camera, since she dressed in her attic bathroom.

He wasn't snooping. He knew how amazing she looked. And he wasn't collecting pictures. Besides, she had a camera on him as part of their agreement.

On screen, she answered the outside door to her attic apartment, not the interior door into the rest of her mother's house. Hercules had used the rickety stairs to that door to visit Dido in the middle of the night. Now it opened to ...

TWO

It took a moment for Hercules to close his mouth and another to take a breath. The tall, tanned, glad-hander Conrad Jackson, their boss, stood in Dido's doorway. He imagined himself not only a network whiz, which he wasn't, but also a chic magnet. He drove a fancy sports car and dressed like a commercial. The jerk was the quintessential one-percenter, taking from those less fortunate than himself.

If it hadn't been for Hercules' mom and his guidance counselor pushing the intern job, and his need to pay for equipment and the exclusive use of his mom's basement, he would have quit in an instant to get away from the ...

Conrad kissed Dido on the lips. She closed the door and dimmed the lights so the bastard's polished TV face faded into shadows. Then she pulled the intruder toward her bed.

Fists clenched, Hercules leaned toward the microphone to tell her to stop. His heart raced. His throat closed. Sweat beaded on his forehead. Blood drained from his face. This was Conrad Jackson, his tyrannical boss, taking everything from him.

"Hercules," Apollo yelled in a computer modulated voice. "You look like you've seen a ghost. You okay?"

"Yeah, yeah." Hercules shook himself away from Dido's image, tried to compose himself, and turned to Apollo's screen. "You got my drill-bit yet?" Hercules referred to the security-penetrating code, and imagined using a real drill on Conrad, right through the forehead.

Dido pulled off her top, revealing her well-toned figure. She'd been working out. Even in the muted light, she looked exquisite, but this wasn't some lame Hollywood movie. He grabbed the microphone. Hesitated. He couldn't give Jackson the satisfaction of knowing he'd gotten the best of his intern.

Even though he couldn't make out much detail in the shadows, Hercules needed it to stop, for Dido to stop. Fear gripped his vocal chords. Not only was he losing her, he was certain she knew of the second camera. Was Dido punishing him for not dropping everything to be with her?

"Look, man," Apollo said without the computerized modulation of his voice. "I'm sorry I yelled earlier. I still think you should give this up. We've thrown everything at their security. Whatever you're digging into is worse than the electrical grid, tighter than the Chinese government."

Hercules couldn't focus on Apollo. He cursed the electronic surveillance that allowed his friend to watch him and considered cutting the feed, but he needed Apollo's toolbox. His guts spun in somersaults. He felt close to his hacker goal, yet was tumbling further from Dido, or she from him. At that moment, he didn't know what to do about Dido. "This is the biggest corporate goon yet, dude," he said to get his mind off Dido.

"Don't kick a hornet's nest."

Apollo didn't have Hercules' passion to chase bad guys. He was doing this for the challenge, and for their friendship. Hercules knew this but they were so close.

Dido's shadowy image pulled off Conrad's tee shirt and dropped her jogging pants. Hercules swallowed hard. His eyes burned. His breathing labored. *Dido?* He didn't know what to do. "The new probe … did you try it?"

"Yeah. It blew back, sliced through my security like a blowtorch on ice. I unplugged before it destroyed my entire network. My computer's a mess. You have to let this go."

Hercules shook his head as a naked Dido pulled the shadowy image of Conrad onto her bed. Hercules wanted to disconnect the video. He couldn't. Most disturbing: she wanted him to see. At least in the faint light he couldn't make out details, and there was no sound.

Dido hadn't promised to be exclusive. He sighed. Actually, she had, but that came with strings: dropping his transparency mission to spend more time with her. He longed to, but he had to do this for Simeon, and to catch bastards like his father who destroyed lives while they hid behind their secret masks. He shook loose from Dido's image, suppressed tears forming around his eyes, and turned to his friend.

"I need you on this," Hercules said, trying to salvage something from the situation. It felt like cowardice.

"I can't help this time."

"Can't or won't."

Dido's enthusiasm drew Hercules' attention. It made his blood boil. Adrenaline kicked in with no obvious outlet. He felt as powerless as trying to break into Krill on his own. Worse. He needed Dido, but with Conrad there, he'd only embarrass himself trying to stop this. He couldn't stop his hands from trembling.

"Stop while you can," Apollo said. "This is the best encryption and counter-hacking I've seen by orders of magnitude. If I didn't know better, I'd say they've figured out how to make a large-scale quantum computer."

Hercules paced, his entire body throbbing in pain. "Quantum? That's gold. Platinum. Supernova. Who are these people?" He willed Dido to stop, but she appeared to have saved up for Conrad. He closed his eyes and turned away from the cameras and screens before he broke down.

"I don't know," Apollo said. "But they're counterattacking. Big time."

Hercules faced his friend. "Do it for Simeon." He sucked in a breath, turned so he couldn't see Dido, and straightened up. "We've made it through four secure walls. I've got a good feeling about this."

"You always do," Apollo said. "We could be peeling an onion or opening the seven gates of hell. Don't forget: we haven't heard from Hades in over a week."

Hercules nodded. Hades was another intern, friend, and the only other member of their team. A week ago, Hercules had asked her to strengthen his code to find a way around Krill's security. Then her camera went dark. She stopped answering texts.

"Hades likes to disappear for weeks at a time," Hercules said. He hoped her disappearance was second thoughts about their mission or a new boyfriend. He dreaded to think he was responsible for making her vanish.

In the shadows, Dido was still at it. With such movement on the squeaky bed, her mom must have gone out. After all, Dido insisted Hercules be quiet while her mom was home.

He couldn't pull himself away, which had him feeling like a wimp. That made him more determined to crack Krill's security system. Girls were unpredictable. Security systems were knowable if you applied the right pressure.

"Hey, man, you seem distracted," Apollo said. "Are you listening? You're not spying on Dido again, are you? Does she know about your second camera?"

Hercules glared at Apollo. He was glad his friend didn't have access to the second feed. He couldn't bear for his friend to see Dido like this.

"Instead of fussing over an impossible security system," Apollo said. "Call her before—"

"It's too late." Hercules slumped into his seat. "She's with Conrad."

"You mean at work?"

"At her place."

"Look, man," Apollo said. "I'm sorry."

"Drop it. Get me the security drill."

"You don't understand," Apollo said. "They messed up my system."

"Zackary," Hercules' mom yelled from upstairs. Hercules cringed. He loathed that name as much as he did one-percenters, polluters, and corporations. He also despised that his mom kept his last name after the divorce. He didn't want to remember his family-wrecking father.

"Come up and eat," his mom shouted in a grating tone guaranteed to rattle his nerves.

Hercules hated her nagging because he lived in her basement. Though not as much as watching Dido still at it. He willed her to stop, but she continued.

Turning away, he caught Apollo with his hand over his mouth, covering the last of his laugh. Hercules' humiliation was complete. Things couldn't get any worse.

Oh, what Hercules would have done for his namesake's strength.

"I'll eat in ten minutes," he promised in a tone he hoped would get his mom to stop.

Apollo was enjoying the exchange too much. Hercules grimaced. It was embarrassing to let his friends see how his mom kept after him, but she wasn't so bad. She let him live in the basement in exchange for paying the utilities, which shot up after he'd installed all his equipment. And she supplied food. But it wasn't cool for Apollo and Dido to see.

"I have to go out, Zackary," his mom said. "Make sure you get some real food."

The nagging was enough to make him leave home, except that required money from a full-time job. He didn't want to work for the man; didn't want a Conrad Jackson boss, a superior bastard with his fancy car and expensive clothes, as if that gave him the right to grab Hercules' girlfriend.

He tried to detach from the screen image of Dido above him, to make this some anonymous "C" rated movie on the dark-net. Then her face appeared from beneath the bastard. Even in the dim light, there was no doubt it was Dido. Hercules could have kicked himself for turning down her invitation.

Clenching his fists, he turned to Apollo's image. "Can you help me with the firewall?"

"I'll have to debug my computer first."

"Then, pretty please?"

Apollo sat at his computer. Dido continued her gymnastics. Hercules returned his attention to his screen.

Something was happening.

* * *

A probe returned, filling three of Hercules' screens with images and data. *I'm in,* he said to himself. *Level five breach,* the message said.

He looked for someone to share this with. Apollo was busy fixing his busted computer. Hercules decided not to disturb him. There was no interrupting Dido.

Symbols filled the screen. One was the FBI emblem. Others included CIA, NSA, and Foreign Service equivalents in a variety of languages, including Chinese and Russian. He'd seen them before in his search for buried secrets. Though never all in one place.

His eyes couldn't take in all the images speeding across his screen. Thanks to the superfast network hub housed in an office building behind his mom's house, download speeds were too fast. That hub was the real reason he stayed in his mom's basement. While she was out, he, Apollo, and Dido had spent two weeks digging a sixty-foot tunnel. Using equipment bought on the dark-net plus Apollo's design additions, they hacked into a satellite hub that connected Hercules' network to the office building's trunk line. But with so much data flowing into his computer, he would have to rely on his system's ability to analyze what it downloaded.

Files spilled across Hercules' screens confirming for him that Krill had the biggest secrets of all. There had to be a conspiracy with so many world governments coming together behind this fishy company. But what did it mean?

Being right felt gratifying. Krill was the ultimate hack. Heart racing, he so wanted to share this with Dido, but she was still sharing with Conrad. Their boss acted like a robot. No, a robot would have been smarter. Conrad was quite human, down to that nasty mole on his backside, made uglier by the dark shadows.

Hercules turned to tell Apollo of his good fortune, but his friend was typing into his virtual keyboard trying to revive Lazarus from the dead. That was what he called the machine that had crashed a dozen times. There was dead, and completely dead, but Lazarus wasn't there yet. Apollo had a knack for resurrecting electronics. Hercules needed his friend focused.

Then all six of Hercules' screens froze. They went blue, the blue screen of death.

"No, no, NO!"

THREE

Hercules looked up to see if Apollo had heard his scream. His friend was deep in concentration, still trying to breathe life into Lazarus. On a separate screen, Dido and the jerk were on her bed. Hercules wanted to puke. Thankfully he had nothing in his stomach, which growled in protest.

The blue screen turned black and then white. Blood-red letters appeared: <Zackary Bakke. Zak-Bak. Labors of Hercules. The mythical Hercules himself. A very naughty boy. Now you caught a bug.>

Hercules struggled to breathe. Dread cascaded over him and something else. He couldn't move his arms. He was pinned to his seat. He flexed his biceps. Nothing moved. He couldn't lift his legs or move his head. His eyes flitted from Dido to the bloody screen.

<You downloaded a nasty virus. It gives me control of your computer. I also entered your motor cortex to put most of your muscles to sleep. Don't worry; it doesn't interfere with heart, breathing, or brain activity. For now, I'll allow you to hear, see, and talk. Otherwise, you've been unplugged.>

Hercules had imagined that things couldn't get worse,

that he'd hit bottom. Now he wasn't sure how much worse they could get. He tumbled in a free fall. His stomach reacting as it had on a rollercoaster, only this wasn't fun. He could only imagine the terror in his eyes.

"Apollo," he yelled to get the dude's attention.

His friend continued tapping furiously at his virtual keyboard.

"Apollo!"

Images flashed across his friend's screen. Hercules was powerless to enlarge so he could read what Apollo was working on. "Look up at my screen." Hercules tried to point. His hand didn't move.

If only he'd gone up for breakfast, this might not have happened. But it had. His mom often checked up on him. She would notice something wrong, but she'd gone out, and could be gone for hours.

He tried to recall what he'd read about psycho-neuro-immunology or some such nonsense about how suggestion could affect reality inside his body and brain. He wondered what words had flashed across his screen to cause paralysis. The online post he'd read talked about how the mind could alter the immune system, but it wasn't a stretch to see how it could affect muscle control, like how voodoo must work. The brain was, after all, an enormous biological computer. He couldn't focus to sort it out.

He grunted. Exertion didn't break the spell. The only thing he could move were his eyes, forced to watch Dido and the death screen. His mind frantically searched for answers. Mostly it swirled in vicious circles as if twisting into a Gordian knot. He couldn't find the end to start unraveling it.

<As you see, paralysis has set in,> the screen read. <You might experience numbness. You will remain conscious until the end.>

That sounded disturbingly final. "Dido, you were right," Hercules said, watching her disturbing image.

"Look at your screen." But she'd turned off her speakers to punish him for ignoring her as Aeneas had done to his Dido.

A thought entered his head. "Computer, sever the web connection."

The icon for the web link flashed green. It turned red with a jagged line to indicate the connection had broken.

Even with the link severed, he couldn't move or shake loose of this nightmare. "Apollo! Look at the screen." His friend didn't shift his attention. "Apollo!"

With his head locked in place, Hercules had full view of all the screens and not much else. He couldn't see the foil bags he'd emptied of snack foods. He couldn't reach his Power drink to keep him alert and quench a growing thirst.

Above him, on the wall, Hades was dark. Dido was in bed. Apollo worked his computer. He might get it fixed. That was a little hope.

"Apollo," Hercules said. "Cut your connection before it's too late."

He prayed for his mom to return. She would march down to find out why he hadn't eaten and help him. But help how? He couldn't explain what had happened. Whoever had hacked his computer couldn't have drugged him through the screen or keyboard. Could they?

The web-disconnect reattached as a single icon and turned green, announcing that the connection had been restored. It copied itself, filling the screen. Then it danced away, followed by images of folders flying out of the two attached hard drives.

* * *

"Helplessness does not suit you." The computer modulated voice sounded male, similar but colder than Apollo's public voice: *a cheap downloaded app.*

The voice continued: "You get this at school, with your internship, and even at home. People bully and boss you around. Bummer. It must grind on you that these people aren't as smart as you. What gives them the right?"

"Corporate pig." Hercules was guessing, though Krill was a good presumption.

"Name calling may squirt dopamine into your brain's reward centers, but it cannot solve your problem. Maybe I can help."

"How?" Hercules asked, and added, "Let me go." His stomach grumbled to remind him of the complete helplessness of his situation.

"What do you think you found?" the voice asked.

"Go away."

The screens filled with the same words in large red letters: <*What do you think you found?*>

"Unleash the Labors of Hercules," Hercules said. He smiled as his defensive bots spread out over the Web following his attacker up the link. *Two can play this game.*

"You have an overdeveloped sense of your own abilities," the voice said.

"And you have a cheap voice modulator. Computer, contact Apollo. Warn him we're under attack. Don't stop until he responds."

"Here, is this better?" The voice now sounded like Hercules' father down to a slight lisp his young girlfriend found cute.

Hercules' paralysis spread throughout his being. Inside, he trembled, which should have been impossible with the muscle block to his motor cortex, but perhaps this was part of his tormentor's plan. His heart raced. He wasn't a hypochondriac, but he felt a heart-attack coming on. "No! Stop it."

"Only you can do that," his father's voice said. "As you see, I reconfigured your computer to bypass your attempt to sever the connection."

"Stop using my father's voice."

"Tell me what you found."

Hercules was unnerved to have his father's voice bearing down on him. He couldn't muffle the sound or move away. He felt another lecture coming from a man whose moral authority ended when he abandoned his family.

"You corporate pigs are hiding something," Hercules said. "Everyone should face transparency."

"So you have no problem with Amanda Jains, Dido, knowing you record her. You could have been with her instead of prying."

"Leave her out of this and stop using that voice."

"Answer my questions first," his father's voice said. The words followed on screen in sharp black letters and lingered.

"What the hell kind of name is Krill Metal Enterprises? Fishy metal. The whole thing stinks."

"You should not have intruded."

"So it *is* a dummy name meant to distract," Hercules said. He grunted to get his body moving. All he managed was to get his heart racing. That realization got his heart pumping harder. "Why does a company with a stupid name, doing boring metal work need tight security?"

"You tell me."

"You have military and diplomatic files. Why?"

"Our IT group has a sense of humor," his father's voice said. "There is nothing illegal about attaching humorous images to boring documents."

"Don't give me that bull. You're hiding something. What illegal work are you doing for the government?"

"We bend things."

"I answered your question," Hercules said, "so stop using that voice."

"You gave me nothing useful. How did you get past five layers of security?"

The Labors of Hercules probes returned, looking bloodied. Red error messages splashed across his screen announcing that the probes themselves had been hacked and left a trail leading back to his computer. These people were good, the best he'd seen. They'd bounced around more foreign locations than Hercules typically used.

A bot returned with the location *Devil's Island*, the French penal colony. That intrigued him as much as the prolonged scene with Dido. Her image pulsed and grew larger as if the screen itself was getting physically closer with its shadowy figures in motion.

Hercules blinked and tried to rub his eyes. Unable to move his hands, he looked away. He wished he'd paid closer attention to that psycho-neuro-stuff as to how to get his muscles working again. He had to figure a way, but it was as if his attacker had drugged him or something. His mind wasn't making connections.

Determined to give up nothing, Hercules stated the obvious. "All electronics use electricity, which is intertwined with magnetism."

To overcome his mental haze, he concentrated so hard he thought he might pass out. He let go and tried to calm himself. This couldn't be happening. It had to be all in his mind. But he would never have conjured up their boss with Dido. *Never.*

"You insult my intelligence," the voice said after a pause. "I am not Conrad Jackson, your guidance counselor, your mom, or, as you surmised, your father. I will, however, get answers. How you answer will determine your fate."

* * *

Fate hadn't been good to Hercules. Aside from his parents' divorce and not fitting in at school, at the internship, or elsewhere, he was sitting at his computer paralyzed. Both Dido and Apollo ignored him. Above them was the silent screen for Hades, and the nagging sense she'd faced the same fate as Simeon. It was Hercules' fault.

"What are you hiding?" he asked. "Espionage? Is that why you have emblems from foreign governments?"

"Souvenirs."

"Not with five levels of security. Computer, send distress messages to Dido and the Labors of Hercules group."

The screen formed the image of Hercules' father, and a simulated mouth moved along with the voice. "If you cooperate, this will go better for you and your friends. Stalling in the hope Mommy will help will fail. She suffered a minor heart-attack and is in the hospital. You should go to her, but until you give me what I need, you will remain paralyzed."

Hercules struggled to breath. His mind clouded. Lack of sleep and food could bring that on. Was he hallucinating? No, the paralysis was real. He couldn't help thinking it was his fault his mom was in the hospital.

She'd supported his computer ambitions, even if she didn't understand them. She'd been more that patient with him. Yeah, it was a plug for independence to complain of her nagging, but not this. In a bizarre way, he missed her nagging, her caring. They should have grown closer after his father bailed. Now Hercules felt guilty about that.

He finally caught his breath. "Leave Mom out of this," he said in a pathetic voice. Then he repeated it as loud as he could.

"You make demands yet offer nothing in return. You need to bargain for what you want."

Hercules' heart fluttered and tightened. Like the proverbial death movie showing all his faults, he saw his mom's support for online classes, days off from school to take network classes, and the grief he gave her like an ungrateful child. He wasn't ungrateful. Yeah, at first he'd blamed her for his father leaving, but the old man was such a jerk and his mom had stepped up to support them.

"Help my mom," Hercules said.

"In exchange for?"

"Heartless jackass."

"Thanks. Now how did you breach our security?"

Unable to rattle his tormentor, Hercules took a deep,

labored breath. He hated the scumbag behind the voice, his father's image on the screen mocking him, and how his friends had abandoned him, turning off their connections so they could concentrate on their own activities. He flexed his muscles. For an instant he thought he detected movement in his right hand. He couldn't be sure. Maybe there was something to the neurological overrides on the brain. He couldn't give up hope.

"Execute Operation Armageddon," Hercules yelled out.

Hercules' computer launched a blast of posts and messages. They were to contacts on the dark-net as well as to friends, a hacker's SOS. They were similar to the last communication he'd received from Simeon, a pre-worded alert that s/he was under attack. The messages would also leave coded clues for Dido, Apollo, Hades, if she was still around, and others. Then his system began a full-scale attack against the last set of code to hit his computer, namely Krill and whoever this clown was, pretending to be his father. Finally, Hercules' system shut down.

"Ouch," his father's disembodied voice said. "You wounded me. The abyss beckons. The end is near."

"Serves you right."

"You have no idea what you are up against. Meanwhile, your mom languishes in the hospital, unable to talk. She has no identification. The hospital has no idea who the Jane Doe is."

"Mom! No." Hercules trembled deep inside his motionless body, probably an echo of the terror in the heart thumping in his chest, growing louder and louder. He tried to push from inside to overwhelm the neural block. He had to get some part of his body to move, anything, but the only thing he could raise was his blood pressure. His heart raced faster and faster.

"Calm down before you injure yourself."

"Swine." Hercules wondered if his tormentor was doing this or if this was a byproduct of the paralysis, the voice convincing his brain that he couldn't move. Maybe he was moving and the block stopped him from seeing this. All sorts of possibilities floated through his head. None of them helped. He took steadier breaths. He couldn't let this money-grubbing scumbag beat him.

"Tell me how you broke into our system and what you found so we can end this."

"Go jump on a live grenade," Hercules said out of frustration.

"Interesting idea. I could place one under your seat to see what happens."

Hercules' eyes watered. It hit him like watching Dido with Conrad. He couldn't believe that in his anger he hadn't pursued this before. He tried to look around. Only his eyes moved, taking in his screens. "How did you get in here to paralyze me?"

"That is your first intelligent question. It will cost you. Answer my question first."

Hercules hadn't seen anyone else in the basement. He only ate food and drinks his mom bought, and he didn't think she would poison him. If anything, she wanted him to finish his internship and go to college or otherwise move out to start his own life.

All electrical outlets were behind computer equipment. If the power behind the voice had jolted him, the flash would have fried the electronics. Not only had his system not fried, it was still up and running, despite his shutdown request. The intruder's control began with the screen, with access to Hercules' network.

"Computer, shut off and don't restart until I give the special code."

The computer attempted to shut down and came back up in a loop. This shouldn't happen. Hercules had built so many redundancies into his system to make this impossible.

"You're wasting time," his father's voice said, matched

by a stern face glaring down. "Meanwhile, the paralysis could become permanent."

"Damn you."

At least with the computer up, he could watch for his probes to return. One might put a stop to this. "I bet they pay you a lot to be a corporate pig," Hercules said.

"Less than peanuts. You and I are not that different, a topic for another time. Despite what you think, time is not on your side. The Department of Defense will be interested in the blueprints you supplied to Chinese agents. You must be desperate to let them go for five grand. They would have paid millions."

"I didn't do it for the money."

"The Chinese used your information to shoot down a surveillance aircraft, killing the pilot and co-pilot. Their deaths are on your head."

Hercules clenched his fists. Only they didn't tighten. He hadn't intended anyone to get hurt. He thought the Chinese having the drawings would prevent a war over control of the South China Sea. Transparency. If he eliminated secrets, no one could use technology to gain a military edge.

"I let the DOD know the Chinese had the blueprints," Hercules said. "It's their fault."

"They won't see it that way. What about the EnviroDyn executive you exposed."

"He covered up toxic dumping. Someone had to stop him."

"Perhaps," his father's voice said, "but when he committed suicide, he killed his wife and oldest son, leaving two young daughters without family."

"It was his fault."

"You could have delivered information to the EPA or the FBI. Instead, you harassed the executive until he killed his family."

Hercules closed his eyes and tried to stop trembling at

yet another reprimand. He'd been unable to sleep for days, wracked by guilt in leaving those two orphans. He was genuinely sorry. This violated his moral code. Perhaps his tormentor was punishment for that, but not in the voice of his father. Hercules had to remove that voice and the face from the screen before he went mad. He swallowed hard. "I didn't hurt his family. He did. Besides, the EPA and FBI are tools of industry. They would have let him off. Computer—"

"You demand transparency from others. Yet you hide behind anonymity in chat rooms in Ukraine, web hosting in Russia, security protocols from China."

"So the nasty bastards can't stop me."

"In other words, hurting people in your drive for transparency is okay as long as transparency doesn't apply to you. What are you hiding?"

Hercules felt pride that he had something this corporate pig didn't have, but that pride faded into his paralyzed condition.

"You believe you have me," his father's voice said. "Hmm."

"Hey, Hercules." Apollo's voice blasted into the room. His face filled one of the screens. "You haven't moved in like forever. You okay, man? I got some weird text about Armageddon."

"Shut off your computer," Hercules said. "We're under attack."

"Can I say I told you so?"

"No! Your computer."

"Computer's still fried," Apollo said. "I got a text on my new wrist-com." He held up the small communication device for Hercules to see. "What's going on? Tell me you stopped probing."

"Apollo. This is the real thing. They've counterattacked. Alert everyone to trace this connection."

"You're nuts, man."

"Do this for Hades," Hercules said.

Apollo threw his hands up. "Okay, don't get so testy."

"Okay," his father's voice said. "You've had your fun."

"Apollo, did you hear that?"

"He can't hear you," the voice said. "I turned off the mike."

FOUR

Hercules' heart tugged in two directions. Part of him wanted to jump out of his seat and ... do what? He wasn't a fighter, not really, at least not face to face. Instead, he hoped his probes might bring something back. The other part of him stewed at the sight of Dido in bed with that jerk. *Will it never end?*

"Hey, Hercules," Apollo said. "Your mike's off. Your mouth moves but I don't hear anything."

Apollo can't hear me. Think. "Computer, send Apollo a text of my conversation with the corporate pig."

"Okay," Apollo said. "Your mike is broken. My computer is restoring itself. I'll send probes to trace who's attacking you."

Good, Hercules thought. *Finally, something's going right.*

"They're taking your Jane Doe into surgery," his father's voice said. The face on the screen grinned with the look of victory.

Hercules wanted to throw up, but that would have dribbled down his front. *Get a grip. That isn't dear old Dad.*

"You're not much for transparency yourself," Hercules said. "Hiding behind my father's image."

"Maybe I paid good money for this face. Your mom is dying. Help me and I will help her."

Hercules swallowed hard: his pride. He couldn't let his mom suffer on his behalf. Maybe it was hard to admit but she had been good to him after his father vanished. "Fine. I'll explain some simple yet useful electronic quirks, but you have to save her. Agreed?"

"If it explains how you broke into our security, your mom will get good treatment."

Hercules would have grimaced but he couldn't move his facial muscles. "When wires run close together, magnetic interference allows signals to jump from one to another. Even well-designed systems pack electronic density so electromagnetic interference becomes a factor."

"You figured out how to use this?" the figure on the screen asked. "Our security walls should have prevented your intrusion."

"My probes figured out where your vulnerabilities were and pulsed signals to bypass your controls."

"How?"

Hercules' face made an effort to smile, but remained a pure poker face. For once, he was glad he couldn't give the jerk the satisfaction of seeing his inner thoughts. "When current hit your barriers, it bounced back and induced signal echoes in nearby circuits."

"Ah, you make use of quantum tunneling."

Hercules felt his face flush. He'd hoped his adversary wasn't clever enough to figure that out. He lacked the resources to build such equipment, but with the help of his friends and code downloaded from the dark-net, he'd developed code that simulated tunneling and induced entanglement to bypass certain controls. "How did your system block this?" he asked. "DOD sites couldn't."

"More requests require that you give more information."

"And my mom?"

"An anonymous caller gave the hospital her name and her doctor's name," his father's voice said. "Now they will make the right decisions. Your mom would be proud of you."

"Damn you."

"Temper, temper. In exchange for your next request, how do we block your probes?"

Hercules refused to give up that tidbit.

"Hey, Hercules," Apollo said, interrupting them. "There's something funky here. Part of the signal runs up that hot line you hacked into the network hub. The rest pumps through your house electrical system."

"Computer, shut off house electricity," Hercules said. He could have kicked himself for not doing this sooner.

Before the lights flicked off, Hercules spotted activity on the lower right corner of the main screen. Chills shot up his spine. His computer had uploaded his entire directory. No wonder the corporate pig kept his computer on. They were stealing his files.

Not anymore.

"Hey—"

That was the last word from Apollo before lack of power shut off the speakers. The room plunged into blackness with only a hint of light from the windows in the furnace room.

"How do you like them apples, you corporate pig?" Hercules' pride faded when he still couldn't move. He hoped his mom would come home; he vowed to have dinner with her every night if she did. But she was in the hospital. His heart ached to go to her. *Sorry, Mom, for all the trouble I've caused you. Please get better.*

Silence was absolute. The air conditioning blower lost its hum. The absent buzz of the electrical panel became ringing in his ears. There were no squeaking floorboards above.

He thought he heard the postman fiddle with the mailbox.

"Hey, help," he yelled. "I'm locked in the basement." He tried to look around. Now he wished he'd installed a camera on the front porch to see for sure. "Hey. Hey. Down here."

He tensed the muscles in his stomach. For a moment, he thought he'd regained movement, but he remained still.

"Help me!"

His voice echoed; then silence resumed. Had he imagined the postman? It didn't matter. There were no more sounds upstairs.

* * *

A short while later the electrical panel sparked. Room lights flickered and came back on. The air conditioner revved up and hummed.

"Sorry to leave you all alone," his father's voice said. "It took a moment to bypass your electrical panel. Enough games. Tell me about electrical vulnerabilities in our security system."

"Get lost, pig."

"You might reconsider before you lose your voice. I warned you paralysis could become permanent."

Hercules grunted. He tried to shout out his protest, but his throat closed. Air puffed out of his lungs, but his vocal chords didn't vibrate. He gasped for breath and exerted himself, trying to get any part of his body to move other than his eyes. Then it hit him. *Paralysis should have stopped eye movement.* That meant this was more sophisticated than a block on his motor cortex. His tormentor wasn't telling him everything.

Panic gripped Hercules until he spotted the hub in the corner by the ceiling. He'd turned it off while he worked on the probes. A light on the experimental gadget was a dull red, almost pink. Hercules stared up, hoping the hub's sensor would connect with his eye focus and turn on.

"Your mom is recovering," his father's voice said. "I kept my end of the bargain."

"Stop using my father's voice," Hercules said, surprised

that his voice had returned.

"Is this better?" The voice switched to his mom nagging.

"No! And why are you stealing my files?" Hercules focused on the hub, hoping the corporate pig wouldn't notice.

"For transparency. You've been holding back."

Hercules expected to have his life flash before him. Instead, he felt like a mouse in a trap, as if the sprung bar was pressing against his spinal cord.

"Apollo! Get over here and turn off the electricity," Hercules said. "Computer, send that message on all frequencies."

The screen before him replaced his father's face with his mom's. In the lower right corner was a note: *Drive A and B files uploaded.* That was all his active data.

One of his probes returned, saying it had reached level seven. He couldn't tell which probe though. *Level seven of what?* He'd reached level five of Krill Metal Enterprises. His only hope was that the probe was digging into the corporate pig and Hercules could activate the virtual hub to view the results as a hologram his tormentor couldn't see.

"Good," Apollo said. "You're back. Did you lose power?"

"Apollo, please. Come over. I need your help."

"He didn't receive your transmission," his mother's voice said. "The connection broke."

"You did it, you money-grubbing scumbag."

"You can't make up your mind, can you?" she said.

"Huh?"

"Scumbag, jackass, pig. Choose one."

Hercules' pulse raced. He had to get rid of this pig. "Okay, you've got my files. Let me go and leave me alone."

"What do you have to trade?"

Hercules had a lot to trade, though he worried that his tormentor had already taken it all.

"Are you not enjoying this hack?" his mother's voice asked. "Is it not as much fun as hacking someone else? By the way, we have all the files connected to your computer and all of your cloud files. Next, we will acquire those locked inside your safe … in waterproof packages covered in aluminum to keep us out."

Hercules turned his eyes far right to see the outline of his fireproof safe. The cabinet was glowing, and not as a reflection of the overhead lights. His chest heaved. His pulse raced. He had to stop this.

"What are you doing to my safe?" he asked. "And how are you doing it?"

"Patience, little Hercules. First, you owe me answers for all the requests you've made."

"You don't get to take things and demand I bargain to get them back."

"Isn't that what you did with the social media company you hacked?" His mother's voice sounded indignant.

"That was different." Hercules stopped before his need to explain himself to his mom got the better of him.

"Good thing money does not motivate you. You could become quite wealthy. Though prison would separate you from your ill-gotten gains."

"What are you talking about?"

"We have a thick dossier on you," his mother's voice said. "Calls to the FBI, DOD, and other agencies and you will disappear into a secure underground facility."

FIVE

Hercules tried to flex his muscles, but only his eyes moved. The hub light turned green. He stared up at the sensors and blinked out two coded, short commands. The first was to notify his Labors of Hercules contacts using a secure channel. The second launched a new probe backtracking on his intruder's connection.

A holographic image appeared before his eyes, announcing that the hub had received his commands and executed them. Simulated mail envelopes flew out of view, moving at the speed of light toward their destinations. After the image vanished, Dido's screen caught his attention. His breathing grew shallow. He was tired seeing the ugly mole on his boss' backside.

Hercules forced himself to look away. The glow in the safe brightened and flashed out.

The darkness stunned him. The corporate pig had taken everything, including evidence Hercules kept as trophies of past successes. Soon there would be no way out of this mess. Who was he kidding? It was already too late. He returned his attention to the image of his mom on the screen.

"Do I have your attention, yet?" her voice asked.

* * *

Hercules could almost imagine his mom putting him through this ordeal as an intervention to shake him out of her cellar. "Go out and meet new friends," she would say. "Find interests outside that computer before it sucks you up inside like a vacuum cleaner."

He wouldn't have minded uploading his brain. That was the dream of singularity; well, of melding the human brain with artificial intelligence. Doing so would allow him to live a thousand years, wandering throughout virtual space, exploring in real time what he could now only do through probes. It was one of his fantasies. His other was to get out of this mess alive.

Hercules wanted more than anything to rewind the day and spend it with Dido. She'd been the best thing to happen to him, not the computer hacks. He could only admit that now because his heart ached so much he could no longer focus on his mission. He tried to tell himself it didn't matter. Why would she want him when she was having so much fun with their stupid boss? That didn't help. Betrayal or not, he wanted Dido back.

"Your mind is wandering," his mom's voice said. Even the lips and facial expressions on the screen were her. "Paralysis is spreading. I can help, if you give me everything."

The hub's holographic image confirmed that it had delivered twelve messages, including to Hades. There wasn't a single reply. What followed would have had Hercules jumping up and down in his seat, if he could. One probe was tracing his intruder's trail all the way to their secure server, sending progress reports along the way. *Got you!*

"Don't count on it," his mother's voice said as if reading his mind. Her face betrayed the haughty look she'd had when she caught him buying equipment he couldn't afford.

"Count on what?"

"I let you play with your hologram. Now it's time to act before you lose your mind. Actually, you will keep your mind, though disconnected from the world. It will not be your upload into the web fantasy. Instead, imagine complete isolation for what seems eternity. Is that what you desire?"

"What else do you want?" Hercules asked. "You have my files."

"That is the correct question. First, what did you learn from our system?"

Hercules felt trapped. "Wait! You plan to kill me after you get everything. You should hire me."

"Why would we do that?" his mother's voice asked. "Your mission is to destroy us."

"You're impressed at how I broke into your system. You could use new talent before someone destroys your little plans."

Mom's face on the screen wrinkled as though thinking. The likeness was unnerving. "Very well. Consider this an interview. Tell me what you learned."

"You mean other than having tighter security than the Chinese government?"

Mom's nod on the screen infuriated Hercules.

"Your first four levels didn't give much," he said. "The fifth had emblems. I swear. I don't have any of your secure files."

"I believe you. We analyzed everything we downloaded."

That shocked Hercules. No one could study all his files in so little time unless ... they had to have a quantum computer. "How did you paralyze me and get into my safe?"

"I could tell you, but then ... you might not enjoy the answer."

The hub light turned red. Hercules stared at it for a long time but couldn't raise its attention. He flashed his eyes past Dido and the jerk to the main screen. His mother's face brushed aside like a dust ball, landing on a side screen. The image scowled at the imposition but didn't say anything.

SIX

In place of his tormentor, an everyman model appeared on the screen dressed in casual business attire. The face was Hollywood attractive, as if advanced photo animation had created the perfectly-dimensioned male face with breeze-blown dark hair and sparkly eyes. The face looked so real it could pop off the screen.

Hercules struggled to move away, to put distance between him and this spooky, all-too-real image. But his body didn't respond.

"My apologies," Everyman said. "Your work triggered our security protocol. You've been talking with our AI agent, Athena."

"I knew it," Hercules yelled. "I knew that creep was no more real than your image."

"I'm Morton Seabrook. You can call me Morse."

Hercules was shaking inside but managed to compose himself. "Release me, you vile swine. What are you hiding?"

"I'm sorry for how Athena treated you," Seabrook said. "She had to be certain you weren't a threat."

"Not a threat? Then why paralyze me? Ah, because I was close to hacking your system."

"Not as close as you'd like to believe," Seabrook smiled graciously when not speaking. "She couldn't be sure without tests."

"What tests?"

"Athena let you believe you could win. She allowed you to send alerts and probes so she could test your capabilities."

"And?" Hercules asked.

"You did better than anyone else we've encountered."

Hercules swelled with pride until he reminded himself his enemy was saying this. "My latest probes confirmed delivery of messages."

"Athena hacked your friends to let you believe you were talking with them. They received none of your messages."

"Now what?" Hercules realized he knew too much for them to let him go. He couldn't escape so he went for another option. "Since you like my work, why not hire me?"

Seabrook grinned and stared at Hercules. "Against Athena's better AI judgment, I'll consider it. You have potential."

Hercules stopped before his anger had him saying something he'd further regret. "To show good faith, release me from this paralysis."

"You've shown no interest in college. You believe you know more than your teachers. You may be right, but you have much to learn. We're prepared to cover your college costs and provide substantially more interesting coursework than you could obtain on your own."

"Wait. You've been considering this all along?"

Seabrook grinned.

"I won't compromise on transparency," Hercules said.

"After you learn what you've been digging into, I hope you'll appreciate how, just this once, secrecy is called for."

"I doubt it."

Hercules looked past mind-numbing images of Dido

and that jerk, to the hub in the upper right corner. It flashed green. A holographic image showed that all his messages had failed. Words formed: *Take the job. It's better than prison, and you'll get to expose bad guys.*

He brushed aside the letters with his hand and stared in astonishment. He could move again. His pulse raced. He stretched, stood, and stretched more, relishing the freedom of movement.

The hub light turned red. Apollo continued tapping on his virtual keyboard. On Dido's screen the mole grew larger as the camera zoomed in, which made no sense. Hercules' porcelain-cat camera didn't have a zoom.

Seabrook watched with that unnerving smile. "I've released the block on your motor cortex. I hope you'll consider our offer."

Now that he could move, Hercules approached the screen and studied the animated image. Anyone could have been behind that face and voice. "Who put you up to this? Conrad Jackson?"

The screen image frowned. "Heavens no. He lacks the mental capacity."

"Then who?"

"You did this by attacking our systems and awakening Athena. Do we have a deal?"

"What about my mom?"

"She's awake and alert," Seabrook said. "Take consolation that in having a minor heart attack today means she'll get proper care before things get worse."

Hercules wasn't so sure. In studying the screen, he considered whether Apollo could have pulled this off. After all, it started after his friend warned him to stop digging. He shook his head. Apollo wasn't clever enough to do this, at least not on his own.

"Take the job," Seabrook said. "You won't be disappointed."

Dido was angry enough to make Hercules sweat, yet neither of his friends could have pulled off the paralysis trick. This had to be someone else. It had to be Krill. Only their level of security could be hiding such an advanced capability.

He didn't see much alternative. Besides the ability to paralyze him, Seabrook had enough information to send him away for good. Taking the job wasn't the worst option. Working for Krill offered access to information beyond anything he'd been able to uncover on his own. Getting into Krill would be the ultimate hack.

Hercules slumped into his seat. "I'll accept on one condition. Tell me how you paralyzed me and took my offline files."

"If I do," Seabrook said, "your security level jumps to level thirteen, meaning you can't share this or other secure information with anyone, not even Dido."

"I doubt I'll hear from her again." Hercules glanced at the screen. Dido and that jerk were going for a Guinness record.

"Last chance. If I tell you, you're bound by our security protocol even if you don't sign up."

"Tell me," Hercules said.

"We have a scaled up quantum computer capable of the levels of security you encountered. Unfortunately, it was vulnerable to quantum tunneling, which you exploited. Thanks to you, we've plugged the hole."

That disappointed Hercules. He wanted to keep digging on his own. "That doesn't explain how you drugged me."

"As a side-effect of the additional computing capacity, we uncovered a different sort of tunneling."

"You've developed a transporter," Hercules said, bouncing in his seat.

"I wouldn't attempt transporting people, too messy. We transmit information that allows us to alter atomic structures and chemical compositions."

"You poisoned me?"

"We rearranged chemicals in your brain to short-circuit your motor controls. We used a similar technique to copy the information on the data drive in your safe."

Hercules tried not to show how intrigued he was. He felt as though he was speaking with Simeon, except the phantom hacker would never work with corporate pigs.

"I hope you can agree that making these blueprints public would be scary," Seabrook said. "We're attempting to locate anyone developing this technology so it doesn't become widespread before we can determine how to control and regulate it. That's where you can help. You asked for transparency. There you have it."

"No one should have this power," Hercules said.

"We agree, but shutting us down won't stop others. Now, I met your condition. Will you join us?"

"Can I have time to think?"

"I'll give you until eight tomorrow morning. You can't tell anyone, not a soul." Everyman vanished from the screen.

Athena also disappeared. The hub light turned green.

* * *

There was a knock at the basement's back door, beyond the furnace room. Hercules answered to find Dido and Apollo, both looking worried.

Hercules stared at Dido, her cinnamon hair windblown around her pale cheeks. Her jogging outfit hugged her athletic figure.

Dido placed her fists on her hips. "Are you going to invite us in?"

"I thought you were with Conrad."

"That jerk? Whatever gave you that impression?"

"Hercules placed a second camera in your room to watch you," Apollo said.

Hercules' face burned. "I'm sorry. I—"

"Save it," Dido said. "What did you see?"

She pushed past him into the cluttered basement and reached the dimly-lit screen where he'd been watching her in bed. Her face turned red. Then she burst out laughing. "You thought that was Conrad?"

"Isn't it? He came to your place today."

"That was last week and I sent him away. I told you."

"Then who is that?" Hercules asked.

Dido pointed to the screen. "Do you really believe I'm here and there at the same time?"

Hercules shook his head. He tried to focus on the dimly lit scene, but he didn't want to see another man's body.

"That's you, you stupid jerk." She punched his shoulder. "That's your mole on your ass. I'm not sure when this was taken, but it's a loop. You see how that bit keeps coming up. I mean, give me a break."

For the first time Hercules studied the ghostly images. He'd seen Conrad enter Dido's room. After that, his image stuck with what was on the dark screen. "I'm sorry," Hercules said, relieved that Dido hadn't been with Conrad.

"You should be, you big oaf. I guess I'm impressed that you cared enough to spy on me. I was beginning to think you didn't give a damn."

"I care, a lot."

"Save it," Dido said. "You've got a lot to make up for."

"So, why did you come over?"

"I spotted your image in a loop, repeating every five minutes."

Hercules opened his mouth to explain what had happened. Seabrook's voice filled his ears. "Tell no one, not even Dido." At first he thought his mind was replaying the warning from earlier. Then he spotted an image on the wall behind his friends, a wall with no screen: *You are under strict security protocol. We'll be watching for your own protection.*

There was something fishy in Seabrook's explanation of the limits of their transmitting technology. It didn't fully explain how they'd reached out and paralyzed Hercules without paralyzing his eyes, but he knew he wouldn't get a straight answer. Perhaps the job would allow him to uncover the real secrets that lay beneath the lies.

The image vanished.

In the corner below the screens was his chess board. Someone had moved the pieces. The only one left in his color was his king in a corner, surrounded by a queen and two rooks, an impossible position during a real game. Triple checkmate.

We'll see about that. This game isn't over.

Hercules smiled. "Let's grab some pizza. My treat." He put his arm around Dido.

She pulled away, went to his keyboard and turned off the looped image of them together. Then she joined him. "Next time, maybe you'll listen to me instead of disappearing into your computer."

Next time.

OTHER STORIES BY LANCE ERLICK

REGINA SHEN: RESILIENCE (Regina Shen book 1)

Outcast Regina Shen is forced by the World Federation to live on the seaward side of barrier walls built to hold back rising seas from abrupt climate change. A hurricane threatens to destroy what's left of her world, tearing Regina from her family.

Global fertility has collapsed. Chief Inspector Joanne Demarco of the notorious Department of Antiquities believes Regina holds the key to avoid extinction. Regina fights to stay alive and avoid capture while hunting for her family. Does she have the resilience to survive?

REGINA SHEN: VIGILANCE (Regina Shen book 2)

Regina Shen is pursued by the notorious Department of Antiquities for her unique DNA. She jumps the Barrier Wall into the Federation to find her kidnapped sister. Stuck on a heavily-guarded closed-university campus in the mountains, she must use her wits to escape and rescue her sister without letting either of two rival Antiquities inspectors capture her.

REGINA SHEN: DEFIANCE (Regina Shen book 3)

Outcast Regina Shen has DNA the Federation believes can reverse a global fertility collapse. Rival Federation agents fight over capturing Regina to gain power amidst turmoil over who will become the new World Premier. Regina has to flee from Virginia through desert and wilderness to Alaska to hunt a treasure big enough to barter for her freedom and that of her sister.

THE REBEL WITHIN (Rebel Series book 1)

Annabelle Scott lives under the iron rule of a female-dominated régime that forces males to fight to the death to train the military elite. When pressed into service as a mechanized warrior to capture escaped boys, Annabelle stays true to herself by helping some escape. Her defiance endangers everyone she loves and thrusts her to a place of impossible life and death decisions.

THE REBEL TRAP (Rebel Series book 2)

Despite being a military recruit, Annabelle Scott rebels against her female-dominated régime by refusing to kill a handsome boy she fancies and helping him escape. Auditory implants and cameras allow her commander to watch her 24-7. Can she help the boy free his brother from a heavily-guarded geek institute without destroying her family or getting killed?

REBELS DIVIDED (Rebel Series book 3)

The first time Geo sees Annabelle, they meet as enemies and she doesn't kill him, which mystifies them both. It's after the 2nd Civil War with the nation divided into an all-female Federal Union and a warlord controlled Outland. The Outland warlord kidnaps Annabelle's sister and kills Geo's father. Can Annabelle and Geo overcome mutual distrust and work together to rescue her sister and gain justice for his father's murder? And will their feelings for each other derail or further their goals?

SHE-DEVIL ROCKS (novelette)

Inspired by *Lord of the Flies*.

Bullied as the smallest of thirteen boys in his class, Bradley is on a plane that crashes on a remote island with a bully who is out of control. Bradley meets a mysterious tomboy who shouldn't be there. He has to learn to survive on the hostile island, deal with the tomboy, and come to terms with the bully.

REGINA SHEN: SALVAGE (novelette)

Living on the seaward side of barrier walls built to protect against rising seas, the only means of survival for Regina Shen is underwater salvage, which is banned by the World Federation. After a storm takes a friend's family and home, Regina is determined to help by defying the Federation

MAIDEN VOYAGE (short story)

Security Chief Nina Rekovic keeps the peace on the all-female Maiden's Ark that left Earth five years before. Distress signal says Earth is lost, stranding lunar colonists. Someone sabotages the vital fertility lab. While balancing Returners she sympathizes with, a dictatorial captain, and an estranged lover who betrays her, can Rekovic solve the conspiracy before she's imprisoned or worse?

WATCHING YOU (short story)

At the intersection of pervasive networks and the Patriot Act, we have the ability and some say the obligation to know everything about everyone. Can privacy survive? Can the individual endure?

Harold is a second-class citizen and a low-level worker in a government surveillance system charged with reviewing "criminal activity." He has private thoughts about a woman he's forbidden from approaching. He will not be deterred.

ABOUT THE AUTHOR

Lance Erlick writes science fiction thrillers for young adult and adult readers. He is the author of *The Rebel Within, The Rebel Trap,* and *Rebels Divided,* three books in the Rebel series. In those stories, he explores the consequences of Annabelle Scott following her conscience. He authored the Regina Shen series: *Resilience, Vigilance, Defiance,* and *Endurance.* This series takes place after abrupt climate change leads to the Great Collapse and a new society under the World Federation. His latest novel is *Xenogeneic: First Contact* about encounters with an alien race aiming to take over Earth.

Find out more about the author and his work at LanceErlick.com. Go to that website to sign up to receive occasional email newsletters with links to free short stories and updates on new releases and other writing developments.

www.ingramcontent.com/pod-product-compliance
Lightning Source LLC
Chambersburg PA
CBHW071214130626
46555CB00004B/1699